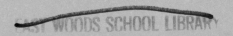

# MAXIMILIAN
## BECOMES FAMOUS

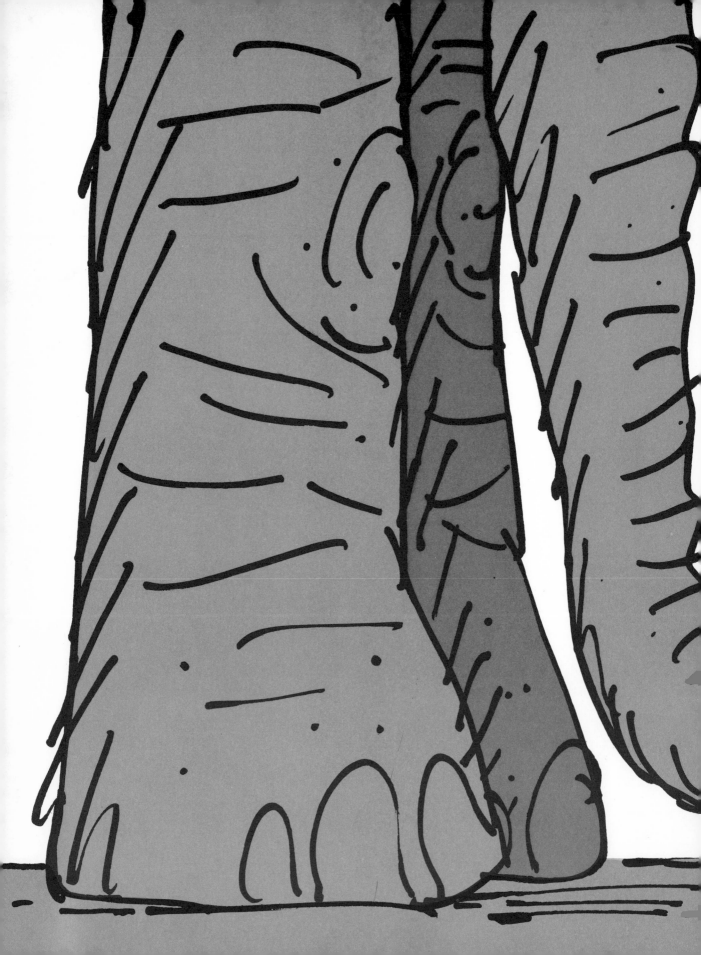

# MAXIMILIAN BECOMES FAMOUS

by Florence Heide

illustrated by Ed Renfro

Funk & Wagnalls / New York

Text copyright © 1969 by Florence Parry Heide. Illustrations copyright © 1969 by Ed Renfro. First published in the United States by Funk & Wagnalls, *A Division of* Reader's Digest Books, Inc. Library of Congress Catalogue Card Number: 70-81922. Printed in the United States of America

1

*to my son David, with love*

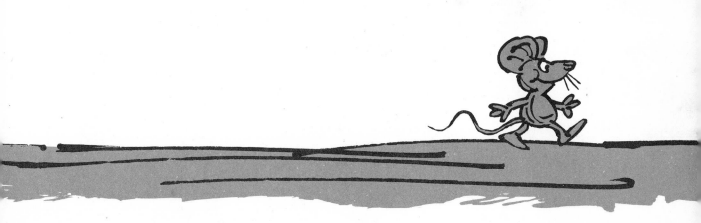

Maximilian and his mother were having breakfast.

"What are mice famous for?" Maximilian asked his mother.

"Famous for? I'm sure I don't know, dear," answered his mother. "ARE they famous?"

"I mean, there must be something that's better about us, or different, or special, or something," said Maximilian.

"Maybe so," said Maximilian's mother. "Do eat more slowly, dear."

Maximilian sighed. "Like giraffes, for instance. Giraffes are famous for long necks."

"So they are," said Maximilian's mother.

"So, what are mice famous for?" Maximilian asked again.

"I just don't know, dear," said Maximilian's mother. "Don't gulp your breakfast, dear."

Maximilian was silent for a moment. "Maybe if I could see what everyone else is famous for, I could find something that mice are famous for," he thought. "Because of course they must be famous for *something*."

Maximilian thought for a while longer. "How could I find out, I wonder?" he asked himself. "Where could I go to see lots of famous animals? Certainly not around here," he thought scornfully. Then he said out loud, "May I go to the zoo today?"

"If you like, dear, but do eat more slowly," said Maximilian's mother.

As soon as Maximilian had finished breakfast, he scampered off to find the zoo. He had never been to the zoo before, but he knew which way it was, anyway, and sure enough, before long he could see in the distance the long neck of a giraffe over the trees.

"I'm glad I don't have a neck that long," thought Maximilian. "It would get pretty boring after the first few days. Even if it does make you famous, I'd rather be famous for something else."

At last Maximilian came to the zoo.

First he came to a hippopotamus.

"Dear me," Maximilian thought as he looked at the hippopotamus. "He certainly is big and ugly."

And big and ugly he was, to be sure.

Maximilian considered. "I guess he's famous for being big and ugly," said Maximilian to himself. "Certainly that isn't what mice are famous for. Not big OR ugly," he thought with some satisfaction as he scampered on.

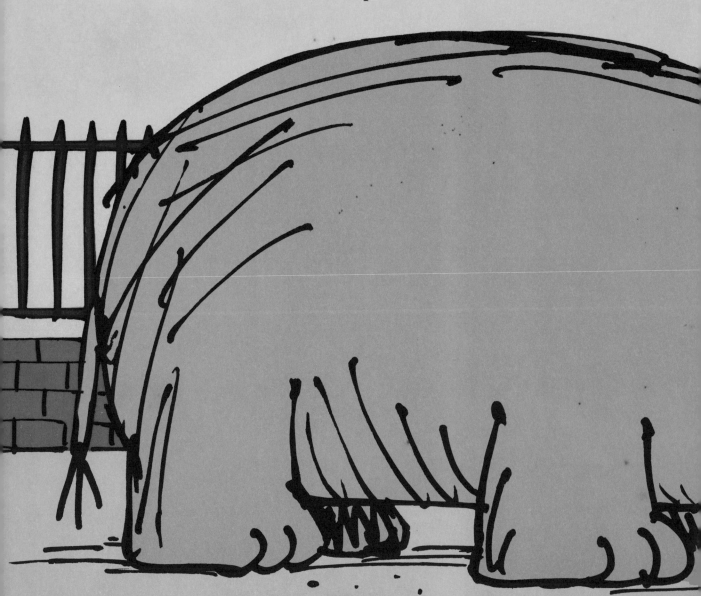

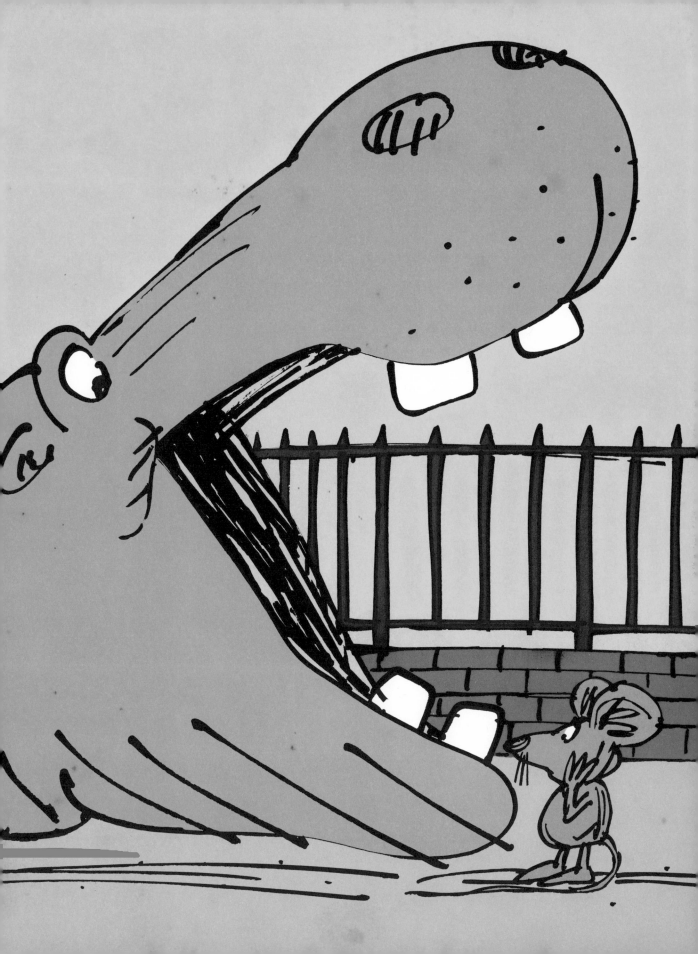

Next he came to a peacock. He knew it was a peacock because the sign said:

PEACOCK
(*Pavo cristatus*)

Maximilian studied the sign respectfully, and then he asked the peacock politely, "Why are peacocks famous?"

"Because they're so beautiful," said the peacock, preening and spreading his tail. "Any fool can see that."

Maximilian sighed. "Well," he thought, "certainly mice aren't ugly, like the hippopotamus, but I'm afraid they're not really beautiful, either. At least," he decided, "not beautiful enough to be famous for it."

"Stare all you like," said the peacock, strutting back and forth. "I suppose you're thinking how beautiful I am."

"What I was thinking about," said Maximilian timidly, "was what it could be that mice are famous for."

"Mice? Famous?" tittered the peacock. "Don't be stupid, Stupid."

Maximilian's feelings were hurt. He turned and started off. "I'm glad mice aren't beautiful," he thought as he scampered on. "Maybe being beautiful makes you rude and disagreeable. Sometimes, anyway."

Suddenly right next to Maximilian's ear there was a loud roar. He stopped in his tracks and looked up. He found himself next to the lion's cage. "Not just the cage," thought Maximilian, "but the *lion*." The lion roared again, and tried to snatch Maximilian with his great paws.

"Goodness gracious," said Maximilian, pulling back. "You certainly are fierce."

"Of course I'm fierce," roared the lion. "That's what lions are famous for: fierceness."

"I can see that," said Maximilian. He thought for a moment. "Certainly mice aren't famous for fierceness," he decided. "Certainly not when they're with lions, anyway," he thought, backing away as the lion roared again.

"Well," thought Maximilian as he scampered on, "mice aren't big, or ugly, or beautiful, or fierce. But what are they?" he wondered. "I know they must be famous for something."

Maximilian ran on until he came to a great shell. A head peered out of the shell and surveyed Maximilian with sleepy eyes.

### TURTLE
*(Chelydra serpentina)*

said the sign. The turtle's eyes drooped. Maximilian thought the turtle might be falling asleep.

"Hey!" called Maximilian. The turtle opened his eyes lazily. "Could you please tell me why turtles are famous?" asked Maximilian.

The turtle yawned. "Because we can pull into our shells when we meet someone who asks boring questions," replied the turtle, pulling his head back into his shell.

Maximilian sighed. "So far I haven't found one thing that mice are famous for," he thought. "At least I'm finding out what they aren't famous for. That's something."

Maximilian stopped to watch the monkeys. They were swinging in the trees and chattering to each other. Maximilian watched for a long time. "Except for swinging around by their tails and looking foolish, there's nothing famous or different or special about them that I can see," he said to himself.

One of the monkeys saw Maximilian and swung over to take a better look.

"What's a mouse doing here, anyway?" asked the monkey curiously.

"Well, I'm just looking around," said Maximilian. "I'm getting ideas about what mice are famous for," he confided.

"Well, what *are* they famous for?" asked the monkey.

"I don't know yet," Maximilian admitted, "but I'm still looking. What are monkeys famous for?"

"Being so human," said the monkey. "See, our faces are arranged just like people's faces. Isn't it silly? YOU don't look like a person at all," added the monkey.

"I know," said Maximilian. "But of course mice are famous for something."

"Don't be so sure," said the monkey as Maximilian turned to go. "If you're famous, why aren't you in the zoo?" called the monkey as Maximilian scampered away.

"Yes," echoed all the monkeys, "if you're famous, why aren't you in the zoo?"

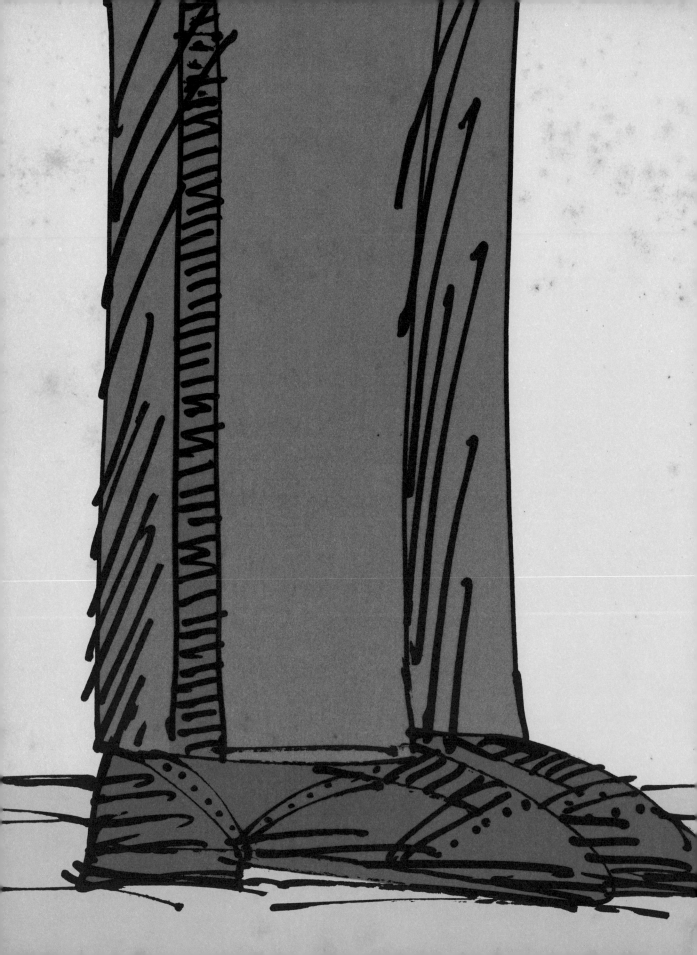

Maximilian ran until he was out of sight, and then he crept along slowly for a while, thinking. "They're right," he decided. "If mice were famous for anything, they'd have one in the zoo. And they don't."

Maximilian sat down, feeling miserable.

He was very, very sorry for himself. "Not for myself," thought Maximilian, "but for all mice. Just think, not one single mouse in the zoo. They're not famous for *anything*, I guess."

He was sitting there still feeling sorry for himself when the Zoo Keeper walked by.

"Hey!" squeaked Maximilian.

The Zoo Keeper stopped. "Eh?" said the Zoo Keeper. "What's this, what's this?"

"A mouse," Maximilian explained modestly.

"So I see," said the Zoo Keeper.

Maximilian cleared his throat. "You don't have any mice in the zoo at all," he squeaked.

"So I don't," said the Zoo Keeper, looking down at Maximilian.

"That must mean there's nothing famous about mice," said Maximilian. "Nothing famous, or different, or special, or anything," he added.

The Zoo Keeper looked at Maximilian kindly. "Maybe I don't have one because I've never had a specimen," said the Zoo Keeper finally.

"I never thought of that," said Maximilian. He frowned. Then he said in growing excitement, "Maybe some things are so famous, or so different, or so special, or so something, that they're hard to get. Maybe that's it," he said hopefully.

"Yes, maybe that's it," said the Zoo Keeper. "And of course this is a very small zoo. We don't get everything. We don't have a Giant Panda, for example."

"You mean," said Maximilian, "you mean, you'd like to have a mouse in your zoo? Because if you would, I could be it."

"Hmmm," said the Zoo Keeper. "A mouse in a zoo? I never thought of that before." The Zoo Keeper peered down at Maximilian a moment. "I'd be the only zoo that had a mouse," said the Zoo Keeper thoughtfully. "I might not have a Giant Panda, but I'd have a Mouse. Why, yes," he went on, "I'd like having you in my zoo if you'd care to stay."

Maximilian paused. "Would I have to stay all the time?" he asked.

The Zoo Keeper considered. "Everyone else stays all the time," he said.

"But I'm not everyone else," protested Maximilian. He thought for a moment. "I'm a *mouse*," he said proudly. "Mice aren't like anyone else. They're different. Yes," Maximilian went on excitedly, "mice are famous and different and special because there is no one else in the world that looks exactly like a mouse, or acts exactly like a mouse, or is exactly like a mouse. Mice are *famous* because they're mice," he said.

"I see," said the Zoo Keeper. "Well, now that you put it that way, I guess you could come and go. We would always keep your cage ready for you. You could easily get back and forth through the bars, you know."

"A cage of my very own?" squeaked Maximilian eagerly.

"Of your very own," promised the Zoo Keeper. "A small one."

"Would I have a sign?" asked Maximilian hopefully.

"Oh, yes," said the Zoo Keeper. "A real sign, just like all the others. Just think," said the Zoo Keeper. "I'll be the only zoo with a Mouse."

Maximilian could hardly believe his good fortune. "Could I just run home now and tell about it?" he asked.

"Oh, yes," said the Zoo Keeper. "You'll be free to come and go. We'll have a nice cage all ready for you any time you get back. We'll try to make it very comfortable. Meals," he went on, "are served at eleven and at four. You may want to arrange to be here at those times."

"Oh, yes indeed," squeaked Maximilian. "I can arrange *that*."

He scampered happily home to tell his mother.

"That's nice, dear," said Maximilian's mother. "You'll always have the cage at the zoo waiting for you, and of course you'll always have your bed at home, too."

Maximilian sighed happily. "Think how famous, or how different, or how special, or how *something* mice must be," said Maximilian, "if they want one of them in a zoo."

"That's true," said his mother. "Don't gulp your supper, dear."

The Zoo Keeper kept his word. Maximilian's cage was always waiting for him at the zoo. And there was a sign on it. A big sign. It said:

MOUSE
*(Microtus pennsylvanicus)*

MOUSE
microtus pennsylvanicus

And of course his bed at home was always waiting for him,
too. And there was a sign on it. A big sign. It said:

MAXIMILIAN
*(Famous for being in the zoo)*